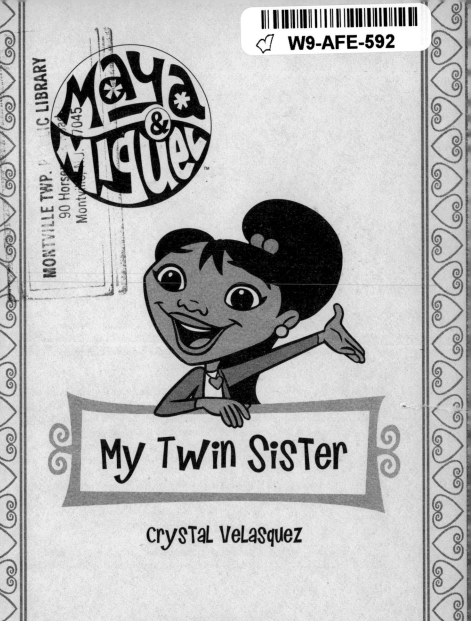

Maya & Miguel™

My Twin Sister

Crystal Velasquez

SCHOLASTIC INC.

New York   Toronto   London   Auckland   Sydney
Mexico City   New Delhi   Hong Kong   Buenos Aires

ISBN 0-439-69603-8

Cover design by Rick DeMonico
Interior design by Bethany Dixon

12 11 10 9 8 7 6 5 4 3 2 1   5 6 7 8 9/0

Printed in the U.S.A.
First printing, April 2005

Every year around our mom's birthday, Maya's gears start working overtime, trying to come up with the perfect present. Our parrot, Paco, might say she gets a little crazy in the head. "*Loca de la cabeza*!" he squawks.

This year was no different.

It all started when Maya and I were in my room, kicking the soccer ball back and forth to each other. The coach said practicing small passes improves your game.

"This year's got to be big!" Maya said

1

brightly as she nudged the ball back toward me. "Mamá's been so busy lately, she deserves a big surprise!" She spread her arms as wide as she could. "*¡Una gran sorpresa!*"

"Maybe we should clean our rooms. Now *that* would be a big surprise," I said, laughing. I turned around and kicked the ball back toward Maya with my heel.

"Ha, ha," Maya said dryly. "I'm serious! It's gotta be something *amazing*, something *unexpected*, something . . ." She scratched her chin and squinted at the ceiling as she absentmindedly shuffled the ball between her feet. Suddenly her eyes shot open and her ponytail bobbed up and down. "Something tropical!" she shouted, kicking the ball so hard that it went bouncing all over the place, rebounding off the bedpost and zooming past poor Paco's head, who ducked just in time.

Maya smiled sheepishly at our parrot. "Oops. Sorry, Paco," she said, and tried to smooth his ruffled feathers. Then the sparkle came right back into her eyes and suddenly her ponytail bobbles glowed. "*¡ESO ES*, Miguelito! Just the other day I heard Mamá saying that she wished she could go somewhere tropical for her birthday. We'll send her to Hawaii! It's perfect!"

Even Paco looked at her as if she had three heads. *Hawaii?* Maybe she really was crazy — *loca*.

"Uh, it's a nice thought, Maya," I said,

"but we'd have to save up our allowance for years to be able to do that!"

"Not a problem," she replied. "I already have a plan."

That's what I'm afraid of, I thought.

Don't get me wrong. I love my twin sister, and her heart's always in the right place . . . but sometimes her plans — well, let's just say they don't quite work out the way they're supposed to.

I remember one time when Abuela tried to teach Maya how to make pancakes. Maya's pancake was a perfect little circle, but when she tried to flip it into the air with the spatula, it never came back down.

See what I mean?

Her plans are sometimes like that pancake. Good, but stuck to the ceiling.

I guess she could see my thoughts on my face. "*Ay*, Miguel, you worry too much," she said. "This plan is going to work. Haven't you been listening to the local radio station? They've been hinting around about a contest all week — and the grand prize is a trip for two to Hawaii! All I have to do is enter and win." She snapped her fingers. "Just like that, we have the best birthday present ever."

"Hmm," I said, picking up the soccer ball and trying to balance it on my nose. I flapped my arms together and said, "Argh argh argh! Check it out, Maya. I'm a seal!"

Maya giggled. "Come on, Miguel. Don't

change the subject. What do you think?" She took the ball off my nose and twirled it on one finger.

"Well," I said, "it's a long shot, but it just might work. I guess it's worth a try."

T he next day, we spent the whole day glued to the radio, listening for details about the contest. Okay, maybe not the *whole* day, but it was a long, long time.

"And that was 'Shelly's Slippery Soap' by the Tongue Twisters," the DJ blared as the song ended. Maya and I grabbed our pencils, ready to write down all the contest information. "I bet you want to know about that Hawaii contest, don't you?" he continued.

We nodded furiously.

"I bet you just can't wait to win, right?"

"Right!" we both yelled.

"Well, I'll tell you how to win . . ."

"*¡Dime, dime!*" we begged, scooting closer to the radio. "Tell me!"

". . . right after these commercials from our sponsors."

"Ugh!" We let our shoulders slump. He'd been saying that for over an hour.

"By the time he tells us, Mamá will have had three birthdays," Maya complained. She sprawled out on the floor.

"Maybe we should think of a plan B," I offered. "You know, in case he never does tell us about the contest."

Maya sprang to her feet. "Good idea!" she said. "How else could we get Mamá to Hawaii? Let's see . . ."

I moved a stepstool to the middle of the room and balanced myself on my stomach. "We could swim there with Mamá on our backs," I suggested, kicking my legs and paddling my arms. I could practically see the blue water all around me. "Look!" I cried. "There's Maui." I spit a stream of salt water from my mouth like a fountain.

"Nice try, Miguel," I heard from above me. I looked up into the clear sky to see Maya with a superhero cape on, flying a few feet above the water. "But I think it would be faster to fly." She zoomed ahead, both arms straight out in front of her. "See you in Hawaii!" she called.

Abuela Elena came in, to find me still balancing on the stepstool, kicking my feet, and Maya standing on the bed, leaning over, with her arms pointed toward the door and a bed sheet tied around her neck. "What are we going to do with you silly children?" she said, putting her hands on her hips. She gathered up some dirty clothes for the laundry, then winked and smiled on her way out. Maya and I looked at each other and collapsed on the floor laughing.

"Maybe we should make those plans Y and Z since they're so farfetched," I said after I had caught my breath.

"Deal," Maya said. "My arms were getting pretty tired from all that flying anyway."

"Aloha!" the DJ yelled. "No more waiting. Here's how you can win that fabulous trip to Hawaii. Write an essay about someone . . . anyone you really care about."

"That's all?" Maya said, dropping her pencil.

"That's all!" the DJ replied.

"Piece of cake!" Maya cheered. "I'll just write about Mamá and how wonderful she is!"

My twin whipped out a glittery notebook and got started right away.

Chapter Three

 "¡P*erfecto!*" Maya said after an hour, giving her notebook a big kiss. "This essay is going to be the grand prize winner! Too bad this isn't for school. I'd get an A for sure."

She shoved it into my hands, urging me to read it. I had to admit, it was pretty good. Anybody who read it would definitely know how cool Mamá is and how much she deserves a vacation. I mean, she's a great cook, she's super smart (especially at math), she's good with animals, and she puts up with Maya and me even when we're cranky. Or worse, hyper! And she has a great sense of humor, which comes in handy when you're raising twins. All of that was in Maya's essay.

"Not bad," I said. "I think we have a winner!" I held the notebook up as if I were showing it to a crowd of fans. I pulled my Frisbee out from under the bed and put it on Maya's head like a crown. Then I held out my fist to my sister like it was a microphone. "So, Maya," I boomed in the same voice the DJ used, "now that you've won the grand prize, what are you going to do?"

"Well, Miguel," Maya said, pretending to dab away tears, "I'm going to give my mother the best birthday present ever and bring about world peace!"

"Fantastic!" I said into my fist.

Maya giggled and playfully pushed my shoulder, then started rummaging around her desk. She came up with a yellow envelope.

"This ought to get their attention," she said. She carefully ripped the pages out of the notebook, folded the essay in three sections, and slid it into the banana-colored envelope. "Let's go mail this puppy!"

"*Squaaaaawk?*" Paco's eyes grew wide.

"Relax, Paco," I said soothingly. "We're not mailing a real puppy. It's just a figure of speech." He sighed and calmed down. "Okay, Maya, let's go!"

Maya skipped all the way down the block

to the mailbox. She looked so happy. A little *too* happy, actually. She just seemed so sure she was going to win. *I'll hate for her to be disappointed if she doesn't*, I thought. Besides, then we'd have nothing to give Mamá for her birthday and we really *would* have to clean our rooms as a present. I shuddered.

That's when I decided to enter the contest, too. I wouldn't tell Maya just yet. I didn't want her to think I didn't have enough confidence in her essay. But it never hurts to increase your odds, right? Right.

So later on that day, when Maya went to the Community Center with Abuela Elena, I took out my notebook and wrote my own essay.

very day after that was the same. Maya would get up early in the morning, get dressed, and run to the mailbox. She would bring in the stack of mail and rifle through it, tossing letters around like a mini tornado. Once she figured out the Hawaii tickets were not there, she'd head to the radio and turn up the volume.

"Today has got to be the day!" she declared for the tenth time.

"You said that yesterday, and the day before, and the day before that . . ."

"But today I mean it!" she said with a smile. I have to give it to my sister. She always stays positive.

"I hope so," I said, feeling pretty skeptical. "We're running out of time." We sat in the kitchen with the portable radio on the table between us. Abuela was by the stove, cooking up some *arroz con pollo*. The smell had my mouth watering! She knows how much we love her rice with chicken. She also knew all about the surprise. After the fifth day of us being glued to the radio, she had gotten suspicious. So we'd let her in on the plan and she promised not to spill the beans.

"Maybe while you wait, you can think about what kind of things Rosa can do when she gets to Hawaii," Abuela said, lifting the lid off the pot and stirring the rice with a big spoon.

"Are you kidding?" Maya said, leaping to her feet. "There're tons of things to do in Hawaii!" Thanks to the reports about the Hawaiian Islands we had to do in school once, we knew all about them. "She can go snorkeling and see all these crazy tropical fish . . ." Maya sucked in her cheeks and puckered her mouth, opening her eyes really wide.

"And they have huge green sea turtles as big as this table," I added, thinking how cool it would be to swim with one. "And don't forget the surfing!" Maya and I immediately struck surfing poses.

"Whoooa!" I yelled.

"Aloha!" Maya sang. We held our hands out with our middle three fingers folded down and our thumbs and pinkies pointed out to the sides.

"See, Abuela," Maya said. "This means 'hang loose' in Hawaii."

To our surprise, Abuela jumped on her imaginary surfboard and balanced on one leg. "*Sí, pero ¿puedes hacer eso?*" she said, winking. Maya and I both tried to balance on one leg like Abuela. We were all laughing and having so much fun that we almost missed it when the DJ came back on and said something about the contest.

"Wait, shh!" Maya said.

"Aloha, all you listeners out there," the DJ boomed. "I've got big news! We have a winner!"

"YAY!" Maya and I screamed.

"I bet you want to know who it is, don't you?"

"Yes! Yes!" we answered him. "*Dime!*"

"I'm going to tell you who it is . . ."

We both scooted our chairs even closer to the table.

". . . in just three days," he said.

"Ugh!" Maya and I put our heads down on the table.

"But I will announce the runners-up, though," he continued. "The lucky winners of the free Tongue Twisters poster and CD are Sandy Delgado, Mark Kawalski, Maya Santos . . ."

Uh-oh.

When Maya heard her name on the runner-up list, she lifted her head slowly and stared at the radio in disbelief.

"*¡Qué bueno, hijita! Estoy muy orgullosa de ti*," Abuela said.

Maya shrugged. "*Gracias*, Abuelita."

"I'm proud of you too," I said. "They even said your name on the radio. Very cool."

"Yeah, you're right," she said and pushed her chair back. "But it still means I have to come up with a plan B for Mamá's birthday."

As she walked slowly back to her room, I could see she was really bummed out about her plan being shot down.

But if I knew Maya, she wouldn't let that hold her back for long.

T hat night I couldn't sleep because Maya was so busy pacing back and forth down the hallway, trying to come up with a new idea. "Think, Maya," she mumbled to herself. "There's got to be something just as amazing as Hawaii or another way to get there."

"*No creo*," I called to her. I chuckled. "If only we could just drag Hawaii here."

Suddenly Maya stopped pacing. Her eyes lit up and her ponytail bobbles flashed brilliantly. "*¡ESO ES*, Miguel! If I can't send

Mamá to Hawaii, I'll bring Hawaii to her!"

I shook my head. Clearly my sister needed some sleep! "Maya, we would need some seriously big muscles to drag a whole island here." I pictured us tying a huge rope around Maui and tugging it across the Pacific Ocean.

"No, silly. I meant that we could turn our apartment into a tropical paradise in time for Mamá's birthday! Picture it."

Hey . . . she just might have something there, I thought. "You mean like maybe we could have some palm trees by the windows?"

"Exactly," she said, starting to pace again. "And we could have coconuts, and leis made of Hawaiian flowers. Maybe we could even cover the living room in sand to make it look like the beach!"

"Yeah," I said, getting into it. "And we could build a small lagoon and fill it with exotic fish. And we'll use the fan to recreate the tropical breeze."

"*¡Perfecto*, Miguel! But don't forget about the music. We'll have Hawaiian songs playing in the background."

"Yeah, and Paco can perch in one of the palm trees."

"Right! *Y comida*. We've got to have a big feast, just like a real luau. We'll need roast pork, poi, salad, macadamia nuts . . ."

As the list grew, I began to have doubts.

It was all starting to sound like trouble to me. Not to mention too much for us to accomplish in a few short days.

"I don't know, Maya," I said. "Can we really pull this off?"

"*¡Claro que sí!*" she cried. "It'll be easy as poi." We both started giggling.

I still wasn't so sure about this, but I couldn't help but admire Maya for never giving up. Even if she was bonkers. Besides, the image in my head really did look like paradise.

"Well, okay. I'm in."

"All right!" Maya cheered. "You won't regret this."

Famous last words, I thought.

Chapter Six

The plan started with cardboard and crayons. Lots and lots of crayons.

First thing in the morning I got to work sketching and coloring in some big palm tree cutouts on the spare boxes we got from the supermarket, while Maya made papier-mâché coconuts.

"How's it going over there?" I called from the floor.

Across the room at the desk, Maya was elbow-deep in flour, water, and newspaper pages. As she slapped the mixture together in a huge bowl, it made a gloppy swishing sound. *Slurp!* Some of it had ended up on Maya's face. "It's going just fine," Maya said, wiping her cheek with her shoulder. "These coconuts will look good enough to eat!"

By the time we broke for lunch, we had two palm trees leaning against the wall and three coconuts drying on the desk.

"Not bad," I told Maya, looking at the coconuts.

"Thanks!" she answered. "It was nothing. And your palm trees . . . wow!"

"Well," I said, raising my chin, "I am an artist."

Maya giggled. "Hey, artist, I just realized something." She looked at her own clothes, then at mine. "We don't look very Hawaiian. We need costumes!"

"Right! Grass skirts and leis coming up."

I pulled out some green construction paper and cut it into long thin strips, then stapled them to longer strips that fit around our waists.

Meanwhile, Maya went to the kitchen to make leis. We couldn't find any real Hawaiian flowers, so she made the leis out of popcorn. She had some to put around our necks and smaller ones to wear on our heads.

When we were done, we looked pretty silly. I wouldn't have wanted my friends to see me like this, but I had to admit I was having fun. *I'll find out how to make Samoan warrior costumes for next time*, I thought.

Maya started to hula dance. "Aloha-hoooo," she sang. "Aloha-hoiii . . ."

I started hula dancing, too. We swung our hips and bumped into each other.

"I need a partner," I said, and grabbed a palm tree. I handed one to Maya and we danced them around the room until we were out of breath.

Maya noticed the clock. "¡*Ay, ay, ay!*" she cried. "Look at the time. I still have to get to the music store to buy a Hawaiian CD."

"And I need to get to the pet store to see if Papi will lend us some tropical fish," I said.

We took off our costumes and set out to finish our plan.

inally, the night before Mamá's birthday arrived. We couldn't wait to see her face when we gave her our present. But we had to ask Papi for help.

"Just get her to go to sleep a little early tonight," we begged him.

Papi looked at us with narrowed eyes. "Hmm . . . first you ask me for some fish, and now this. What are you up to?"

We both shrugged and said, "*Nada*."

"Nothing, huh?" He crossed his arms and

raised an eyebrow.

"Okay, okay," I confessed. "It's a surprise for Mamá's birthday. We just need time to set up for tomorrow." His face broke into a smile and he agreed to help.

After Mamá and Papi had gone to bed, Maya and I brought out our creations one by one.

"This is going to look amazing," Maya gushed. She placed the coconuts on the floor.

"Definitely," I said, leaning the palm trees against the wall.

"Hey, what happened to the lagoon?"

"Oh! Almost forgot." I ran back into the room and came out with a small fishbowl with a lone goldfish inside. "*Aquí está.*" At her look of confusion, I explained, "Papi didn't think it would be a good idea to move the tropical fish, so I borrowed Andy's pet goldfish, Soggy."

She shrugged. "Close enough."

"And where's the Hawaiian CD?" I asked.

"Oh!" She slapped her forehead and came out with a steel drums CD. "It was the closest thing the music store had," she offered and smiled nervously.

"Close enough," I said.

We set everything up and stood back to admire our work. The palm trees were both crooked and bent way over to the side, as if they were exhausted from too much hula dancing. The coconuts were still pretty wet and smelled like paste. Plus, the fish bowl didn't exactly look like a tropical lagoon, and Abuela had said no way to the sand. So it wasn't perfect, but if you used a little imagination (or a lot), it didn't look half bad.

Chapter Eight

T he next morning we got up bright and early to finish setting up. We were so excited that it felt like Christmas morning. We even snuck around on tiptoe so we wouldn't wake up our parents.

Together we lugged the heavy fan to the other side of the room, so it would face Mamá when she entered. Then I went to get Paco and perched him on top of one of the coconuts.

"You're part of the big birthday surprise,

Paco!" I whispered.

"SQUAAWK! *¡Sorpresa! ¡Sorpresa!*" he said way too loud.

"Shh!" Maya and I said at the same time, snapping his beak shut. "Not yet!"

Maya went into the kitchen and came out with a tray full of grapes, pineapple slices, and iced tea. Turns out we didn't have time to roast a pig and make poi. But fruit and tea would be just as good, we thought. Finally, we were ready.

"Wake up, Mamá! It's time to celebrate your birthday!" we yelled.

Mamá and Papi shuffled into the room in robes, still rubbing sleep out of their eyes. "*¿Qué pasó?*" Mamá asked drowsily.

"*¡FELIZ CUMPLEAÑOS!*" Maya and Paco screamed as I turned on the fan. "Happy birthday! Welcome to Hawaii!"

Too bad the fan turned out to be way more powerful than I'd expected. Mamá had just started to look around when the wind from the fan hit her full force and her hair went flying back. I tried to turn it away from her, only to aim it right at the coconuts, which started rolling across the floor — one of them with Paco still attached!

"*¡Ay, qué lástima!*" Maya cried, and went chasing after the runaway coconut that had birdnapped Paco. She caught up to it and pried Paco's claws out of the papier-mâché. "Sorry, Paco."

Paco walked away with his claws sticking to the floor. "*No me gustan las sorpresas,*" he grumbled.

Maya looked at our parents and turned red. "Wait! I almost forgot!" She reached for the steel drums CD and brought it over to the stereo. But her hands were covered in the gluey mess from the coconuts so the CD stuck to her hand. "Oh no!" she cried.

I turned the fan off, but it was too late. The coconuts had left three wet trails all over the living room, the palm trees had fallen on their sides, and Mamá's hair was standing straight up. Our Hawaii was no paradise. It was total chaos.

ChapTer Nine

Maya hung her head down, the CD still stuck to her hand. I could tell she was embarrassed and pretty upset that our tropical dream was ruined. But then we heard Mamá's voice. Wait a minute. Was she . . . laughing?

"*Vengan aquí, mis hijos,*" she said happily, calling us over into her open arms. She hugged us so tight I could hardly breathe. Then she kissed each of us on the tops of our heads. "You two are so sweet to try to do this for me. I love it! I'm very touched." She started to tear up a little.

"Okay, Mamá," I said. "Don't go getting all mushy on us."

"She can be as mushy as she wants today," Maya countered. "She's the birthday girl!"

That night, after we cleaned up the remains of our version of Maui, we threw a little birthday party in our apartment. Abuela made her famous *empanadas con queso y con carne*, and flan for dessert, Mamá's favorite.

"*¡Qué sabroso!*" Mamá told Abuela.

Everything really was delicious. We even let Paco eat one of the popcorn leis for being such a good sport.

Then we turned off all the lights as Papi came into the room, carrying a big chocolate birthday cake, filled with candles.

"Make a wish!" Maya urged. Mamá took a deep breath and blew as hard as she could. All the candles blew out, then lit right back up! She gave a sly smile to Papi. Trick candles. His favorite. We all laughed and tried to help Mamá blow out the candles. Abuela finally took them out and ran them under some water.

Later Mamá opened all her presents. Papi gave her a beautiful red dress and Abuela gave her a pair of shiny gold earrings.

As we watched her open the gifts, Maya still looked upset.

"What's wrong?" I asked.

"It's nothing," she said. "I just wish we

could have made her real birthday wish come true."

An alarm went off in my head. Oh no! I totally forgot about the radio contest! We hadn't listened to the radio all day and tonight they were announcing the winners!

Chapter Ten

I ran over to the radio and turned it to the right station. They were playing a fast *bachata* song.

Papi held out his hand to Mamá. "May I have this dance?"

She agreed and they started dancing around the room. They looked so funny in the grass skirts Maya made them wear.

As the song ended, the DJ came back on the air. "Aloha!" he boomed again. "The moment you've been waiting for is here — we are announcing the grand prize winner of our Hawaiian vacation essay contest!" They played a drumroll in the background followed by a loud cymbal crash. "The winner is . . . MIGUEL SANTOS!"

"Woo-hoo!" I yelled, pumping a fist in the air.

Maya's jaw hit the floor and her eyes bugged out like one of those puffer fish in Papi's pet store.

"Shh!" the DJ said, as if he could hear me. "I want to read some of the winning essay. It's all about how his twin sister Maya tried to win this contest as a present to her mother. Isn't that sweet? Now listen up: 'Every year around our mom's birthday, Maya's gears start working overtime . . . '"

"You wrote about me?" she asked.

"I just wanted to back you up, just in case."
I winced, hoping she wouldn't be upset.

"That's so cool!" She jumped up in the
air, then hugged me almost as tight as Mamá
had.

"Hey! I'm not done yet!" the DJ
interrupted. We quieted down. "All of us
here at the station thought the essay was so
good, we're throwing in three extra tickets
so the whole family can go!"

"Even me?" Abuela asked.

"Even Abuela!" the DJ responded. Weird
how he seemed to be listening to us, too! We
all started jumping up and down and hugging
each other. Paco flew over our heads yelling,

"Aloha! Aloha!" I was thrilled to see how excited Maya and Mamá were. Their smiles were a mile wide.

"Now we can give you a great present after all!" Maya told her.

"Oh, *mija*," Mamá said. She squeezed the stuffing out of Maya, then called me over to put an arm around me, too. "I've never gotten a better present than my twins."

$O600856$

TM

Mexico City   New Delhi   Hong Kong   Buenos Aires

No part of this publication may be reproduced in whole or in part, or stored
in a retrieval system, or transmitted in any form or by any means,
electronic, mechanical, photocopying, recording, or otherwise, without written
permission of the publisher. For information regarding permission,
write to Scholastic Inc., Attention: Permissions Department,
557 Broadway, New York, NY 10012.

ISBN 0-439-69603-8

Cover design by Rick DeMonico
Interior design by Bethany Dixon

12 11 10 9 8 7 6 5 4 3 2 1   5 6 7 8 9/0

Printed in the U.S.A.
First printing, April 2005

Chapter One

My brother Miguel is pretty great — and I'm not just saying that because he's my twin. I really mean it! He's smart, he knows tons of knock-knock jokes, and he always brings me back to Earth when I get too excited about an awesome idea. Well, most of the time, anyway. But I guess no matter how great you are, sometimes you can forget. Good thing I'm around to remind him!

The first bell of the day had just rung as I watched Miguel set up a small table in front of Mr. Nguyen's class.

"Um . . . Miguel?" I asked, flipping through

the giant stack of index cards piled on the table. "How many oral reports are you giving today?"

My friend Maggie, who stood next to me, giggled, and poked a small model of a building with one of her fingers. "And what is this?"

Miguel swiped the index cards from me, then shooed Maggie's hand away. "That happens to be a scale model of an Aztec ruin from the city now known as Cuernavaca."

"Oooh," Maggie and I said sarcastically. *"Aaaah."*

"Now, now, ladies." Miguel held up his hands the way the crossing guard does when she wants us to wait on the corner. "I know it's hard being around someone so brilliant, but try not to let it get to you. As you will find out today, I'm just an average, ordinary genius," he said, and then

ran his hands through the sides of his hair and flipped up his shirt collar. And he almost did it with a straight face! We were all laughing by the time Mr. Nguyen came into the classroom, carrying a load of books and papers.

"This is it," Miguel said, unfolding a big poster board with an Aztec culture timeline on it. "Time to knock everybody's socks off."

"Or at least their shoes!" I joked. "*Buena suerte,* Miguelito."

"Thanks, Maya," he said, and then turned to our teacher. "Good morning, Mr. Nguyen. I'm all ready to give my report —"

"Oh, Miguel," Mr. Nguyen interrupted. "Would you mind if we held off on that? I have an announcement to make to everyone."

"Oh, uh . . . sure," Miguel said. He gathered

up his stuff and went back to his seat.

"All right, everyone, settle down," Mr. Nguyen called, clapping his hands together to quiet us — which isn't easy to do, let me tell you! "We have a new student joining our class today." He motioned for the dark-haired boy who had been standing by the door, quiet as a mouse. The boy walked over and looked out at us while Mr. Nguyen told us to make him feel welcome. "Go ahead and introduce yourself," he encouraged the new boy, who cleared his throat and swallowed so hard you could hear a big gulp!

"Hi, everybody," he started nervously. "Uh . . . my name is Carlos Márquez."

"HI, CARLOS!" the class yelled. We all started laughing.

That broke the ice and Carlos finally cracked

a smile. "I just moved here from Japan, where my dad was stationed with the Marines. Before that it was Brazil, and before that Italy, and before that Egypt . . ." Carlos scratched his head. "Well, it's a long list." Miguel and I looked at each other with our mouths hanging open.

"Cool!" Miguel whispered.

"Anyway, I'm glad to be here," Carlos said. "I hope I get to stay for a while."

For a second the class was completely silent. Then all of a sudden it was like we were at the Super Bowl — the crowd roared! Everyone surrounded Carlos, exploding with questions. "What was school like in Japan?" "Have you been to the pyramids in Egypt?" "Did you see any soccer matches in Brazil?" The teacher tried to get us under control, but we were just way

too excited. I mean, having a new kid in class is always fun. But in Carlos's case, it was extra fun because he had lived practically everywhere!

I was heading toward Carlos myself to ask if he had any exotic pets — like maybe a llama! — when I glanced over my shoulder to see Miguel staring down at his index cards. He shoved them into his backpack. In all the commotion, I had forgotten about Miguel's big moment in the sun.

"Hey, Miguel," I said. "Sorry you didn't get to give your report today."

"That's okay." He strained his neck, searching through the crowd. "Maya, can you believe how cool Carlos seems? I've got to go welcome him to the class. I bet we'll be great friends!"

"That's the spirit!" I said. Before I even got the sentence out, Miguel had cut through the crowd to

introduce himself to Carlos. They shook hands.

"If you need somebody to show you around," Miguel said, "I'm your man."

"Great," Carlos said, looking relieved. "I was afraid I would go looking for the bathroom and end up in the janitor's closet by mistake!"

Miguel laughed. "Don't worry," he told Carlos. "I'll show you the ropes."

Later that day during lunch, Miguel and I went looking for Carlos. "*Ándale*, Maya," Miguel said, snapping his fingers as we rushed through the lunch line. "If we don't hurry, we won't get to welcome Carlos to our table." I could tell Miguel really wanted to be Carlos's friend. And you know me — I just wanted to help any way I could.

"Okay, okay," I said, grabbing a small bowl of grapes to put on my tray. "Keep your shirt on." But by the time we got to our usual table, Carlos was already sitting there, surrounded by half the class. Miguel's smile faded a little. It looked like

he wasn't the only one who wanted to be friends with Carlos.

I nudged him in his side with my elbow. "Come on! Once Carlos hears how much you have in common, you guys will be fast friends." We had to squeeze onto the bench like a couple of sardines.

"Hey, guys," Theo greeted us. "Good timing. We were just telling Carlos about the soccer team."

"Are you going to join?" Miguel asked Carlos, hopefully. "If you want, I can give you a few pointers after school."

"Yeah," I chipped in. "With his help, you'll be up to speed in no time!"

"Sure, thanks," Carlos said. "I hope I'm good enough."

"Good enough?" Andy piped up. His blue eyes were as big as basketballs. "He lived in Brazil for a year, remember?" he said to Miguel. "Soccer is huge there. He probably has a million moves he could teach us!"

Miguel and I both looked at Carlos, who just shrugged and said, "I'm an okay player. But I still have lots to learn."

"Well, you might as well get started today," I declared. "In fact . . ." My ponytail bobbles started glowing as I came up with a great idea. "*¡Eso es!* Miguel, why don't you show him some of your signature Santos moves now?"

"Um . . . now?" Miguel asked, giving me that raised-eyebrow look that means, *Have you gone bonkers*?

"Sure, why not now?" I continued cheerfully.

"Earth to Maya," Chrissy said. "We're in the lunchroom and we don't even have a soccer ball."

"True!" I said, holding up an index finger. "But all we need is a little imagination." I held out a grape to Miguel. "Here's your soccer ball. And here," I said, spreading my hand over the table, "is the field."

"Ooh! And here is the goal!" Maggie cried, getting into it. She held up two straws at the end of the table.

"I'll even play defense," I offered, my two fingers running up and down the "field" like a tiny pair of legs.

"Okay, you asked for it," Miguel said with a big smile, walking his own fingers toward the grape. And the game was on! Everyone cheered as he

kicked it left, trying to get around my hand, but I blocked and sent the grape rolling back toward him. Then he faked left, faked right, and kicked it right past my fingers, right between the straws and . . . *SPLAT!* . . . right into Mr. Nguyen's face, who was sitting across the aisle, talking with some other teachers. Oops!

"Hey!" he yelled, wiping the smashed grape off his cheek.

"Sorry, sir," Miguel mumbled and tried to disappear into the bench.

Everybody thought it was pretty funny, but I could tell Miguel was embarrassed.

O n our way home after school, Miguel looked a little bummed out. *"¿Qué haces?"* I asked him.

"Nada. It's just that Carlos has played soccer in Brazil," he said, opening his arms, "while all I showed him was how I could hit teachers with grapes."

"Well, sure, when you put it that way, it sounds silly." I tried not to giggle. I glanced sideways at Miguel, covering my mouth. At first he gave me a huffy look, but then he started giggling, too.

"I guess it was kind of funny," he said. "We could call it the Great Grape Escape."

"Hey, that's pretty good!" I said.

"Carlos is just so cool," said Miguel. "I think we'd be great friends. But he probably thinks I'm a big goof now."

"Hey, no one thinks you're a goof," I replied. "But maybe there is something you can do to impress Carlos."

"Uh-oh, *hermanita*. Sounds like you already have a plan."

"Who, me?" I replied, batting my eyelashes.

Miguel crossed his arms and looked me right in the eye. "Yo te conozco, Maya. Yo sé cuándo tienes una idea. Your ponytail bobbles are lighting up the whole block!"

Oh! My ponytail bobbles always give me away. "Okay, you're right. I do have an idea. I thought maybe you could jazz up your report. You have

to give it next week, right?"

"Yeah," Miguel said suspiciously. "And it's done already. But . . ."

"Pero ¿qué?" I asked.

"Well . . . it's good," he said quietly, "but it could be *great!*"

"Then how about we ask Mamá to help us put all the pictures in your timeline on the computer?" I suggested. "Then you can show them to the class on Mr. Nguyen's computer like a slide show!"

Miguel scratched his chin. "You know, I hate to admit it, but that's brilliant!"

"What can I say?" I replied, fluffing up my ponytail. "Genius must run in the family. Now, what are we waiting for? Let's get started!"

We hurried home to ask Mamá for help. *"Esa es*

una idea muy inteligente," she said. "I've already started doing that with your baby pictures. See?" She popped in a disk and showed us picture after picture of Miguel in a T-shirt and diapers, sucking his thumb, and being fed mashed peas.

"Awww, *Miguelito*," I gushed. "You were so cute! But Mamá, where am I in all these pictures?"

Mamá laughed. "We could never get you to sit still long enough to pose with your twin," she replied.

Miguel covered the computer screen with his hand. "Just make sure my friends never see these, Mamá," he said. "I'd never live it down!"

"No te preocupes, hijito," Mamá said in a baby voice and pinched his cheek. She put in a blank disk and showed Miguel how to turn his poster board into a slide show.

Chapter Four

Finally the day came to present the rest of the oral reports. Maggie paced the length of the classroom like a nervous cat. "Relax, Maggie," Miguel told her. "You're making me dizzy." He crossed his eyes and let his tongue hang out the side of his mouth.

"Besides, you look fantastic, Maggie!" I added. She was doing her report on the Japanese tea ceremony and was wearing a traditional kimono.

"Thanks," Maggie said. "I'm just glad I won't be up there alone!"

Right then, Carlos joined us. "Ready when you are," he said to Maggie.

Maggie explained that since Carlos could speak a little Japanese, Mr. Nguyen was letting him help Maggie with her project.

"Wow, he can speak *three* languages. That's so cool!" Miguel whispered to me as they set up in front of the class.

I nodded. Carlos *was* pretty cool. But I couldn't wait for Miguel to show everybody that he was pretty cool, too.

The good news is Maggie's report was awesome. Carlos did the whole ceremony in Japanese, and Maggie handed out real tea to the entire class. *¡Delicioso!* Everybody cheered.

Then came Miguel's turn. "Here you go," I said, handing Miguel a disk. "You almost forgot it this morning!"

"*¡Ay, ay, ay!* Thanks, Maya," Miguel said. "What

would I do without you?"

He went up and showed the class the scale model and read his index cards. Then Miguel turned on Mr. Nguyen's computer that sat facing the class, and put in the disk. "These are the ruins as they look today," Miguel said.

Instead of the ruins, slide after slide of Miguel in diapers began flashing across the screen. The class started laughing like crazy!

"Nice outfit, Miguel!" Maggie called with a giggle.

I must have grabbed Mamá's disk by mistake!

Miguel's eyes bugged out of his head. He tried to get the disk out, but it was stuck!

And there's Miguel sucking his thumb, I thought, *and Miguel sleeping with a fuzzy teddy*

bear . . . I looked over at Carlos. He was laughing pretty hard, too! What a disaster!

Good thing Miguel never panics. He walked back to his seat and brought back the trusty poster board and planted it right in front of the computer, blocking the screen. Pretty soon the class calmed down and paid attention again. I put my head down in relief. I was sure that my brother would forget all about this mess instantly.

"I am never going to forget about this, Maya!" Miguel said later that night in my room.

I winced. "It wasn't *that* bad, was it?"

"Not that bad? *Not that bad?*" I could almost see the steam coming out of his ears.

"Okay, so my plan didn't go quite right today. *Mil perdones, Miguel.*"

"*Squaaawk!* Sorry a thousand times!" Paco translated, landing on Miguel's head.

Miguel sighed and let his shoulders slump. "That's all right. I know it was just an accident. But Carlos must think I'm a total goof now —

showing off my baby pictures."

"Hmm . . ." My brain zoomed in all kinds of directions. "There has to be some way to show him how cool you are . . . *¡Eso es!*" I cried, leaping to my feet. "Tomorrow we have a big soccer game. That's your chance to show Carlos your *real* signature Santos moves. You know, without the grapes."

Paco perked up. "Grapes? Paco likes grapes! *¡Dame uvas!*"

"Sorry, Paco," I said. "We were just talking about something that happened before." He let out a disappointed *"bwak"* and settled back down on Miguel's head.

"I guess you're right," Miguel agreed. "I could totally impress Carlos on the soccer field."

"Especially if you come up with some brand-

new, out-of-this-world move!"

"Yeah!" Miguel said, getting excited. "I'm going to do something so incredible tomorrow, Carlos will definitely want to be my buddy!"

"All right!" I cheered, giving him a high five.

The next afternoon, there we were on the field with the clock running down. Our teams were tied and one more goal on either side would definitely win the game. As much as I wanted my team to win, I kind of hoped Miguel, on the opposing team, would finally get his chance to shine. Oh, I wouldn't make it easy for him, but if I knew my brother, he would find a way to take the ball and score the winning goal.

The ref counted down and suddenly the ball was in play. It zoomed around the field so fast, I almost lost track of it. It bounced off of one girl's

knee, then Miguel dribbled it for a while, zipping past a bunch of players.

I had to fight the urge to cheer for him. Then the ball came my way. I was determined to get it back downfield toward the other team's goal. But just as I had the ball in perfect position to send it flying across the field, one of Miguel's teammates swooped in and stole it from me, kicking it right to Miguel. He was all by himself and I knew it was time for his new move. He started to do some kind of fancy spin and swung his leg up in the air, but I guess the grass was a little too wet, because he slipped and landed on his back with a thud.

"Oof!" both he and I gasped at the same time.

Meanwhile, the ball rolled toward the out-of-bounds line. That's when Carlos came flying

out of nowhere and got to the ball just in time. He flipped it into the air with his foot and head-butted it right into the goal! It was unreal! You could hear the coach on the sidelines yelling, "Goooooooaaall!" The whole team was wowed by Carlos's amazing play and started chanting, "Carl-LOS! Car-LOS!"

Eventually Miguel got up and chanted, too, but I didn't think he'd ever try that move again.

After the game, the whole team took Carlos out for pizza to celebrate the big win.

"Carlos," Miguel said, standing up, "I raise my pizza slice to you."

"To Carlos!" the team yelled, raising their slices. Everybody took a big bite.

"Ah, it was nothing, just a lucky shot," Carlos mumbled.

"Oh yeah?" Andy said. "Well, we could use a whole lot more lucky shots!"

As we were leaving the pizza shop and everybody started to head home, I turned to

Carlos. "Hey, I never got to ask you if you have any pets." I was still hoping to hear about a llama.

"I wish!" he said. "I move around way too much to have a pet."

"Well, then, you should come by my parents' pet store this Sunday," Miguel offered. "We have more pets than we know what to do with!"

"Really? *Sí, gracias.* That would be great!"

I knew Miguel was just trying to be nice, but bringing him to the pet store was a perfect idea! We had just gotten the cutest new beagle puppy and Papi said she was crazy about people. All I would have to do is hand her over to Miguel in front of Carlos and the puppy's cuteness would do the rest.

That Sunday, Carlos showed up bright and early. "*Bienvenido*, Carlos," Mamá said to him.

"I've heard so much about you. Please make yourself at home."

"Gracias, señora Santos," Carlos answered politely.

"Now, who wants to help me clean out the dogs' cages?" Mamá asked.

"I do! I do!" I volunteered. Miguel gave me a funny look. We loved the dogs, but cleaning out their cages wasn't much fun. He knew I was up to something. "What? I just love puppies," I explained.

"If you say so," Miguel said. He started sweeping the floor of the shop. Mamá and I began with the older dogs, and after the third or fourth smelly cage, I was ready to quit. Pee-eeew! But when we finally reached the puppies, it was all worth it.

The little beagle was so adorable! She had white fur with a brown nose and big floppy ears. She stood on her hind legs with her tiny paws against the bars of the cage, her tongue hanging out.

This plan would work even better than I'd thought!

While Mamá went outside to take out the trash, I lifted the puppy out of the cage, holding her away from me. She wriggled and squirmed like a fish! "Miguel, can you hold this one while I clean out the cage?" I asked.

"*¿Por qué no?*" he answered. Why not?

As soon as he brought her close to his neck, the dog went crazy licking his hands and his face.

"Wow! She really likes you!" I said.

"Yeah," Carlos added. "You're good with animals."

Miguel couldn't help smiling, even though the wriggling puppy wouldn't sit still for a second! "I guess —"

But just then, the cute little thing wriggled free and jumped right out of his arms.

Oh, no!

She was too young to control her legs properly, so she bumped into everything.

The beagle leaped onto a stack of fliers we had piled by the door and they scattered everywhere.

Then she slid on a piece of paper and went skidding into a table leg.

The table she bumped into was the one with all the birdcages on it, and all the birds went

wild, screeching and squawking and chirp-chirp-chirping.

That, of course, got the dogs barking.

Miguel chased after the puppy, accidentally knocking over an empty fishbowl that broke and poured water out all over the floor. Finally, he trapped the beagle between the iguana tanks and the hamster cages. "Gotcha!" he said, and quickly put the little rascal back in her now clean cage.

Too bad the rest of the store was a complete wreck!

"Whoa, this place is like a rodeo!" Carlos said, smiling.

Mamá came back in and just stood there, staring at the floor. *"Ay, ay, ay,"* she said. "What's gotten into you kids?"

"Lo siento, mamá," I said. "We'll clean it up." I whispered to Miguel, "Sorry. I just wanted to show Carlos your special talent with animals."

"Ha! Nice try," Miguel said. "But my only special talent seems to be making a mess!"

Chapter Seven

After that, Miguel made it very clear that he didn't want to hear any more of my "brilliant" ideas.

"What about if we —" I began.

"No way."

"But not even if —"

"Uh-uh. Forget it." He clamped his hands over his ears.

"All right, all right," I said. "But just for fun, I still think we could have done something *big*!" I opened my arms as wide as they could go.

Miguel stood on a chair. "Like maybe I could walk to school on stilts and tell everybody I grew

five feet overnight!"

"Now you're talking." I smiled. "Or you could learn some magic tricks and make all of our schoolbooks disappear!"

"Hey, you could have something there," he said, grabbing a black hat and a pencil. "Hocus pocus, gobbledy-goo . . . send our books to Timbuktu!"

I rolled on the floor, cracking up. "Or you could become an astronaut and wave to us from the moon!" I bounced around the room like I was weightless.

"Is it me," Miguel said, bouncing around the room, too, "or does this place look like Swiss cheese?"

"What?" I shouted. "I can't hear you through this big glass helmet I have on." I patted the

imaginary circle around my head.

Miguel laughed. "Well, those are all pretty big dreams, and you never know what's going to happen. Maybe I will be Spaceman Santos one day. But for now, I'm just Miguel, and I've got homework to do."

"Okay," I said, taking off my space helmet. "But are you sure we can't try just one more thing?"

"Maya . . . " He crossed his arms. *"¡Por favor, no más ideas!"*

"Whatever you say," I agreed.

But no more ideas? That would be tough!

I was back in my room doing my homework when all of a sudden my ponytail bobbles started to glow.

¡ESO ES!

Miguel said I couldn't come up with a plan, but he didn't say anything about *Abuela*!

I quickly ran across the hall to Abuela's apartment.

I explained the whole thing to her as I sat at her kitchen table. I hadn't seen Paco all day so I'd brought him along, too.

"What should we do, Abuela? I just want everybody, especially Carlos, to see how special

Miguel really is."

Abuela slid a plate of *buñuelos* in front of me. Mmmm. I loved it when she made that Mexican dessert. "And how were you planning to show everyone that?" she asked.

"Well, maybe we could shoot Miguel out of a cannon during half time at the next soccer game," I suggested. "He could do three somersaults in the air, and then land on his feet like a cat!"

Abuela just blinked at me, then shook her head.

"No, you're right," I said. "Where would we get a cannon? Hmm . . . maybe I could enter Miguel in a professional skateboarding tournament so he could show the pros how it's done!"

One look at Abuela's face told me that wouldn't work either.

I munched on another buñuelo while I thought. "Maybe we could show his drawings in the community center, like a real art gallery. Oh! Or he could try breaking a world's record in something, like walking on his hands!" I jumped up and did a handstand in the kitchen.

Abuela caught my legs before I went tumbling over.

"Maya," she said, holding my ankles in her hands. "Do you really think Miguel needs to do any of these things to prove he is special?"

I looked up at Abuela. I could see right up her nose! "No?" I asked, unsure. "I just thought we needed to think big!"

She let go of my legs and told me to sit down. "*Mijita,* Miguel is special because of the kind of person he is, not because of what he does,"

said Abuela. "He just needs to be himself. *¿Lo entiendes?*"

"*Creo que sí,* Abuela."

"I think so! I think so!" Paco screeched.

Abuela was right as always.

A few days later during lunch, Miguel and I went to sit at our usual table. Carlos was already there, but he looked downright mopey.

"What's the matter, Carlos?" Miguel asked, sitting next to him.

"Yeah, why so glum, chum?" I added. "Why so gloomy, Gus?"

That made him smile, but just a little.

"My father just heard that he'll be stationed somewhere else in a few months. I'm going to have to move . . . again." He played with the mashed potatoes on his plate, moving them from

one side to the other.

"Oh," Miguel and I said at the same time. Now we were all Gloomy Guses.

"I really don't want to go," Carlos continued. "You guys are so much fun! You're the coolest kids I've met so far."

"Really?" Miguel asked, sounding shocked.

"Really!" Carlos replied. "And now I have to leave. I'm never in one city for longer than a year and it's hard *always* being the new kid. You guys are so lucky. You've all been friends for years!"

"Hey," Miguel said, squeezing Carlos's shoulder, "who says just because you're moving that we can't still be friends?"

"Yeah," I agreed. "You're not leaving the planet, are you?"

Carlos chuckled. "No," he answered. "But I'm

probably leaving the country."

"So?" Miguel said. "Even if we can't hang out in person, we can do the next-best thing. We'll be e-mail pen pals!"

"E-mail pen pals?" Carlos repeated. "No one's ever offered to be e-mail pen pals with me before."

"Well, now someone has," Miguel said, offering his hand to Carlos. They shook on it, and then exchanged addresses. "Maya and I will keep you in the loop so you'll always feel like part of the gang."

Carlos didn't know what to say, but he certainly wasn't gloomy anymore. And boy, did he dig into those mashed potatoes!

I'd never been prouder of my brother. He was really cool, even without holding the world's

record for walking on his hands.

I told him so as we walked home after school. "I figured it out, *Miguelito*."

"What's that?"

"The way you care about everybody and make *them* feel special makes you a pretty amazing guy."

"Aw, Maya," Miguel said, his neck turning red. "Do you have to be so sappy?" But then he smiled and said, "Thanks."

All of us stood in front of our building in a circle around Miguel — Maggie, Chrissy, Theo, Andy, and of course, yours truly. Carlos had moved to Spain a week ago and Miguel had gotten his first e-mail. We couldn't wait to hear what Carlos had to say. Paco sat on Miguel's shoulder, looking down at the printout in his hands.

"'Spain is great,'" Miguel read. "'Tell Theo I haven't seen any bulls yet, but when I do, I'll be sure to take a picture.'"

"Don't forget to run right after you see one!" Theo shouted.

"*¡Toro!*" I said, holding out my red jacket.

Paco flew at it, but I lifted it just in time. "*¡Toro! ¡Toro!*" he repeated.

Miguel laughed and continued. "'I've already met a couple of people here, but it doesn't compare to hanging out with you guys. I'm so jealous that you get to stay there with all your friends, Miguel.'"

Miguel finished reading the letter, then looked around at all of us. "I really am lucky," he said.

"Hey, everybody, get against the wall so I can take a picture and attach it to our next e-mail to Carlos," Chrissy said, removing her digital camera from around her neck. "I have a timer so we can all be in it." She set the timer and rested the camera on a fire hydrant while the rest of us scrambled into position. "What should we say?"

she panted as she ran into the shot.

"There's only one choice," I said, smiling at our friends.

Just as the picture snapped, we all shouted, "HI, CARLOS!"